ASHA and BAZ
Meet Elizebeth Friedman

The ASHA and BAZ Series
Don't miss out!

ASHA and BAZ
Meet Elizebeth Friedman

(Book 3)

By Caroline Fernandez

Common Deer Press

Published in 2023 by Common Deer Press
1745 Rockland Avenue
Victoria, British Columbia
V8S 1W6

This book is a work of fiction. All incidents and dialogue, and
all characters, with the exception of some well-known historical
and public figures, are products of the author's imagination and
are not to be construed as real. Where real-life historical or public
figures appear, the situations, incidents, and dialogues concerning
those persons are entirely fictional and are not intended to depict
actual events or to change the entirely fictional nature of the work.
In all other respects, any resemblance to persons living or dead
is entirely coincidental.

Library and Archives Canada Cataloguing in Publication

Title: Asha and Baz meet Elizebeth Friedman / by Caroline Fernandez.
Names: Fernandez, Caroline (Blogger), author.
Description: Series statement: Asha and Baz ; book 3
Identifiers: Canadiana (print) 20230153119 |
Canadiana (ebook) 20230153127 | ISBN 9781988761831 (softcover) |
ISBN 9781988761855 (EPUB)
Subjects: LCSH: Friedman, Elizebeth, 1892-1980—Juvenile fiction. |
LCGFT: Time-travel fiction. | LCGFT: Fantasy fiction.
Classification: LCC PS8611.E7495 A94 2023 | DDC jC813/.6—dc23

Cover and interior illustrations: Dharmali Patel
Book Design: David Moratto

Printed in Canada
CommonDeerPress.com

*In honour of Elizebeth Friedman and all
women in science and technology
who overcome challenges to make
amazing discoveries.*

Kaavya, your happiness is your strength,
Always keep smiling. You are perfect the way
you are. You're an amazing individual and
I am proud to be your mom.

CHAPTER 1

THE CODEBREAKER CHALLENGE

"How do you write a secret message without using invisible ink?" Ms. Wilson giggled as she asked the class. Everyone looked around at each other. When their teacher laughed that way, it meant she was up to something fun.

"Does this have anything to do with a class challenge?" asked Asha. She was the most curious kid in the grade.

"Yes!" exclaimed a thrilled Ms. Wilson. "It's the Codebreaker Challenge!"

"Chal-lenge, chal-lenge, chal-lenge," the class chanted.

"Pick a partner and get into teams," directed Ms. Wilson.

Everyone settled into their teams. Asha and Baz picked each other, as always. They were best friends.

"So, how do you write a secret message without using invisible ink?" asked Ms. Wilson.

Hands shot up around the class. Ms. Wilson pointed to each person, giving them a chance to speak.

"Use a picture instead of writing a word," suggested a girl.

"Write the message in a different language," said a boy.

"Use numbers instead of letters," Baz whispered to Asha.

"Baz says," Asha said, "use numbers instead of letters."

Baz sunk down in his seat.

"Thank you, team Asha and Baz," replied Ms. Wilson. Baz was grateful she didn't force him to speak up for himself.

"I think you will like this challenge," said Ms. Wilson. "It's about secret codes and codebreaking."

Ms. Wilson walked to the front of the class. She began writing on the blackboard.

CODEBREAKING: science, history, engineering, math, AND solving puzzles

- Replace letters with numbers
- Replace letters with symbols or pictures
- Use different languages or alphabets
- Replace numbers and letters with dots and dashes

"Secret codes are so much fun," said their teacher. "Long ago, kings and rulers sent messages written in secret code. That way, no one could steal their messages," Ms. Wilson explained. "We still use secret codes today. Can anyone think of a secret code?"

Hands shot up all around the class.

"My computer password," said Asha.

"Barcodes on cereal boxes," suggested a boy.

"My mom's four-number secret code for her bank card," suggested a girl.

"I LOVE this brainstorming!" replied Ms. Wilson. "You are all correct."

The class cheered.

Ms. Wilson took a stack of worksheets from her desk and started handing them out to the students.

"The team that solves the Codebreaker Challenge gets a reward," announced Ms. Wilson.

"A reward! What is it?" asked a girl.

"You have to crack the code to find out. It's hidden in the secret message," replied Ms. Wilson. "Read the instructions."

Baz tapped Asha's arm. She bounced up and down in her chair.

"A reward," Asha whispered in his ear.

"We have to win this," replied Baz.

The class fell silent as they read the instructions.

The Codebreaker Challenge

Instructions: Solve the letter/number key below to decode the secret message.

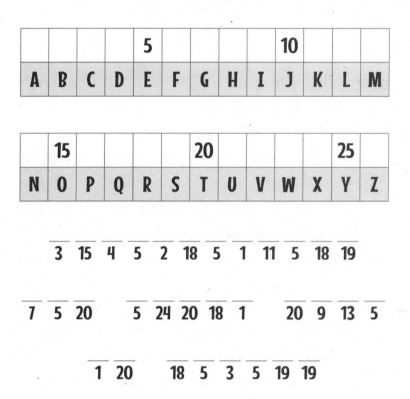

				5					10			
A	B	C	D	E	F	G	H	I	J	K	L	M

	15				20				25	
N	O	P	Q	R	S	T	U	V	W	X	Y	Z

3 15 4 5 2 18 5 1 11 5 18 19

7 5 20   5 24 20 18 1   20 9 13 5

1 20   18 5 3 5 19 19

"It looks like math," Asha whispered to Baz. "No," said Baz, looking at the worksheet. "There are no addition, subtraction, or other

5

math symbols." He read the instructions out loud. "Solve the letter/number key below to decode the secret message. We have to figure out how the numbers and letters work together. See how some of the letters already have a number?" he said as he pointed to the page.

"5, 10, 15, 20, 25," Asha read out loud.

Ms. Wilson walked up and down the rows of desks. "You need to find the *key* to unlock the code," she hinted. She clapped her hands together with excitement. "Now that you've had a look at the challenge, get ready for recess. When you come back, you can jump in to puzzle-solving."

Everyone in the class stood up and walked toward the door. Asha pulled Baz to the side and whispered in his ear, "I'll get the magic stick. You bring the worksheet, OK?" Baz doubled back to his desk to get the worksheet. Meanwhile, Asha went over to her backpack and took out a strange-looking stick.

At that moment, the recess bell rang out.

The kids walked down the hall and out the back door to the schoolyard. Once outside, Asha and Baz broke into a run. Asha carried the magic stick, and Baz clutched the worksheet.

They raced down the hill and past the soccer field. They ran to where the grass turned into sand. That's where they stopped.

Asha looked over at the worksheet. "OK, so we need to crack the code," she said. "This time you use the magic stick." She held out the stick to her friend.

Baz took a step back and looked at her with worry. "No, no, no. I don't want to be the one in charge of the stick," he protested.

They had found it in the schoolyard. It was not the regular kind of stick one would find lying around a playground. No, this did not fall off a tree. Someone had created this tool. It was a dark brown color at its base that flowed into a honey color at its tip. And it had a strange bend in the middle. Asha and Baz were both drawn to this stick...for this was a magic stick.

"It won't hurt you," said Asha. She held the magic stick out for Baz to take.

He bit his bottom lip and shook his head. He held up the worksheet instead. "No, Asha," he said. "I don't want to hold the magic stick. I'll hold the worksheet."

"Are you sure? It's OK if you want to have a turn with it," said Asha.

"I'm sure," Baz replied.

Asha knew Baz was a worrier. On the other hand, she was fearless. "I understand," she said.

"Can I see the worksheet, please?" she asked.

Baz held out the paper. They looked at it together.

"Ms. Wilson said we have to find the *key* to unlock the code," said Asha. "It's a hint!"

Asha bent down. Using the magic stick as a pencil, she wrote the secret message in the sand.

3 15 4 5 2 18 5 1 11 5 18 19

7 5 20   5 24 20 18 1   20 9 13 5

1 20   18 5 3 5 19 19

"Step in," Asha invited Baz. Baz stepped into the drawing next to Asha. Next, she pressed the tip of the magic stick to the sand. "Codebreaker," she yelled. In that exact moment, the south wind blew sand into a gentle tornado around them. Asha and Baz were transported through space and time.

8

The mini tornado blew away as quickly as it had blown in. Asha and Baz looked around. The playground and school were gone. Instead, they were standing in someone's yard.

"The secret code!" Baz exclaimed, pointing at the ground.

It was magic.

There, in the sand, the numbers were gone, and in their place was a name and a year:

ELIZEBETH FRIEDMAN. 1942.

CHAPTER 2

1942, Washington D.C.

Asha and Baz were standing in a small patch of sand in front of someone's house. The air was warm, but not hot. The sky was blue. The grass was thick and green.

"This house doesn't look modern," said Asha. "The magic stick has sent us back in time to 1942. To meet someone named Elizebeth Friedman. She must know about codebreaking."

"Where do we find Elizebeth?" asked Baz. He looked around the yard. It was empty.

"This must be her house," said Asha. She put the magic stick in her pocket for safekeeping. "Let's go knock."

They walked up the stone path to the brick house. Asha and Baz looked up. There were five windows on the second floor and four windows on the first floor. The path led up to the front door.

Baz stopped at the door. "You knock," he said, pushing Asha forward.

"You are going to have to get over being shy one of these days," warned Asha.

"I know," he said. Yet, the thought of being the one to knock made him feel like he was going to throw up.

Asha knocked three times.

The door opened.

"May I help you?" asked a woman.

Her black hair was in a low bun. She was dressed in a gray blouse with a black cardigan over it. Her black skirt went down to her ankles. She wore black shoes with thick heels.

Baz gave Asha a tap on her shoulder, signaling her to be the one to talk for them both. "OK, fine," Asha whispered to Baz.

"Excuse us for bothering you," Asha began. "We are looking for Elizebeth Friedman."

"Are you the two new trainees?" she asked.

Baz replied without thinking, "No, we're—"

Asha elbowed him in the ribs. "Yes, ma'am," she said. "Yes, we are the new trainees."

Baz knew what to do. He followed Asha's lead.

"Yep, we're the new trainees," he said.

"You look a little young to be trainees," said the woman. She looked Asha and Baz up and down.

Baz bit his lip as he always did when he was nervous. Asha did not miss a beat. "You can't judge a book by its cover," she replied.

"You are right about that," said the lady with a smile. "Things are not always what they seem. What are your names?" the woman asked.

"I'm Asha, and this is Baz," Asha replied.

"Hello, Asha and Baz. Yes, I'm Elizebeth Friedman. Welcome to your first lesson in codebreaking." She stepped to the side and invited them into the house.

CHAPTER 3

WORLD WAR II

Elizebeth led them inside. To the right there was a polished wooden staircase going up to the second floor. To the left there was a living room. Elizebeth led Asha and Baz down a narrow hallway between the stairs and the living room.

"In here." Elizebeth held out her hand to invite them into the room at the end of the hallway.

The room was bright and tidy. There was a white brick fireplace. A family picture hung above the fireplace. Beside the fireplace was a large white, wooden bookshelf built into the wall. Someone had organized all the books.

Asha walked to the books. She was a curious girl. There were plays, reference books, science books, and more.

"Have you read all these books?" Asha asked.

"Not all," Elizebeth responded. "The science books belong to my husband, William. What types of books do you like to read, Asha?"

"I like fiction books," she replied.

Elizebeth smiled. "William likes fiction too."

She turned to see Baz still standing in the doorway. "What types of books do you like to read?" she asked.

Baz's cheeks flushed hot. "Nonfiction," he said.

"I also like nonfiction. Why don't you join us? I don't bite," Elizebeth said.

Baz walked into the office and joined Elizebeth and Asha.

"Can I ask a question?" Asha asked.

"Of course," Elizebeth replied.

"Why are you codebreaking in your house? Shouldn't you be working in an office somewhere?" Asha asked.

"Good question, Asha. Yes, codebreakers

work in offices. And I used to. But since I had my family, I've been working from home," said Elizebeth.

"Doesn't your mom work from home?" Asha asked Baz.

"Yes," he mumbled.

"Let us begin," said Elizebeth. She reached under her desk and took out a black leather case. She unlocked the case and took out some papers. She laid the white, crisp sheets of paper on the desk for Asha and Baz to see.

"What is your previous experience in codebreaking?" Elizebeth asked.

Asha and Baz looked at each other. "You speak," Baz said to Asha.

Asha sighed. She shook her head at Baz.

"We know there are different ways to write secret messages," said Asha. She thought about their secret message class with Ms. Wilson. "For example: using pictures instead of words. Or using different languages." She couldn't remember the last example. "What was the other one?" Asha asked Baz.

Baz pressed his hands together. He didn't feel comfortable talking in front of new people. And Elizebeth was new to him.

"Using numbers instead of letters," he said in a shy voice. He avoided looking Elizebeth in the eye.

"Well then," said Elizebeth, "you are off to a good start! Codebreaking numbers instead of letters is exactly the type of codebreaking I am working on."

Elizebeth took a seat at the desk, while Asha and Baz leaned in.

"I have broken many secret codes over the years. Some codes take weeks to crack," said Elizebeth.

"Oh no," groaned Asha. "Will it take us weeks to solve the code?" Codebreaking didn't sound like action and adventure at all. It sounded like hard work.

"No, this code won't take us weeks," replied Elizebeth. "I've been working on this one for some time already. I am close to cracking it."

The three codebreakers looked down at the papers. The top of each sheet read TOP SECRET ULTRA. There were double-spaced rows of typed numbers. Some numbers had pencil circles around them. Elizebeth had written notes on the sides of the pages.

Baz was just starting to read the notes when there was a knock at the front door.

Elizebeth gathered up all the sheets and put them back into the black leather case. Then, she locked it.

"Stay here," she warned. She hid the case back under her desk.

Asha and Baz peaked out from the doorway. Elizebeth answered the door. There was a man in a military suit standing there.

"He's Navy," Baz whispered to Asha.

"How do you know?" asked Asha.

"I've seen pictures," he said. "White hat, gold buttons, and blue suit. That's someone from the Navy."

They listened to Elizebeth and the Navy person.

"Have you broken the code yet?" the Navy man demanded. He was taller than Elizebeth. His face was serious. He stood very straight. He pushed his shoulders back to look even bigger.

"He looks like a bully," Asha whispered to Baz.

"He looks scary to me," Baz replied.

The Navy man held a black leather case in one hand.

"As I've told you before, Captain, it takes time to break a code," Elizebeth replied.

"We don't have time, Mrs. Friedman. This is top priority!" he said.

"Then, you should give me today's messages. And let me get back to my work," she replied. She pointed to a black leather case. He frowned. He looked left and right to be sure no one was watching. Then, he handed over the case.

"My future depends on you cracking this," he said in a low voice. "I want to get out of this unit and get a job at headquarters. As soon as possible!"

"I know," she replied. She sounded fed up. "You have told me before. Many times." Elizebeth closed the front door before the Captain could say another word.

"We're in 1942, right?" Asha whispered to Baz.

"Yes, that's what the magic stick wrote in the sand," he replied. "Why are you asking?"

"Because it's 1942! Don't you remember what happens in 1942?" asked Asha.

"World War II starts in 1939. America joins the war in 1941," said Baz. "So, in 1942, the world is at war."

That is when it hit him. "Secret messages in

1942 must have something to do with World War II."

"Exactly!" said Asha.

At that moment, Elizebeth walked into the office.

"Today's messages," Elizebeth said, unlocking the Captain's black leather case. It looked exactly like the other case hiding under her desk. She took out the new papers.

TOP SECRET ULTRA was on every page.

"Are these spy messages?" asked Asha.

"Yes," Elizebeth replied, sitting down at the desk.

"So, since we are in America," Baz guessed, "we must be working for the Americans to break Nazi codes?" Baz remembered that the Nazis were the bad guys, in charge of Germany during World War II.

"We *could* be doing that," Elizebeth answered. "But my work is secret. I don't even share what I work on with my family."

"Where is your family?" Asha asked.

"My two children are at school. And William is at work," Elizebeth answered.

"Does your husband know you are a spy?" Baz asked.

"I'm not a spy. I'm a codebreaker," Elizebeth

explained. "I don't create secret messages and I don't send them. I only solve them."

"Did you have to go to school to become a codebreaker?" Baz asked with interest. He didn't feel as shy as before.

"Pull up some chairs," Elizebeth said, "and I'll tell you how I got into codebreaking."

CHAPTER 4

CODEBREAKING

Asha and Baz dragged two wooden chairs from the dining room and set them in front of Elizebeth's desk.

"First," said Elizebeth, "there is no school for learning how to break codes. I taught myself how to do it. I trained my husband to be a codebreaker too, but William and I work on different projects. And we never discuss our work. It's very secret."

Asha's eyes went wide. "You taught yourself? You must be good at math."

"It isn't just math," Elizebeth said, shaking her head. "Codebreaking also requires logic, asking the right questions, and spotting patterns."

Asha scrunched up her face, looking confused. "Spotting patterns?" she asked.

"Yes, seeing the repetitions or similarities beyond the chaos," Elizebeth explained with a smile. "Here, let me show you."

Elizebeth walked over to the bookshelf. She reached up to the top shelf and brought down a box. It was a puzzle box. She returned to the desk, opened the box, and showed the contents to Asha and Baz.

"Imagine you have one hundred puzzle pieces," Elizebeth explained. "We know they join together to make a picture. When the pieces are not put together, it's a mess." She pointed to the pile of puzzle pieces in the box. "But then, we start to find patterns." She sorted through the pieces until she found two that each had a bit of red on them. "And we can start putting pieces together." She connected the two pieces. "See," she said with a smile, "now it's coming together."

Asha and Baz clapped.

"So, to break a code we have to find patterns and put pieces of a puzzle together bit by bit," said Baz, understanding Elizebeth's example.

"That's it!" Elizebeth approved.

"How did the government find you?" Asha asked.

"So, you think I work for the government?" Elizebeth asked Asha.

"I guess," said Asha.

"Well, your guess is correct," said Elizebeth.

"Oh, I've worked in codebreaking for a while now," she said. "During World War I, I broke codes for the government. Then, I worked for the police. After that, I was in charge of a codebreaking unit for the U.S. Coast Guard. But that unit moved to the U.S. Navy. That's why the Captain visits me every day." Elizebeth nodded to the front door. "Now he's in charge. But I'm the one doing the codebreaking."

"He seemed kind of grumpy," said Asha.

"He wants a different job," said Elizebeth, "and he thinks breaking this code will get him that job."

"Will you get a new job if you break the code?" asked Baz.

"Oh no. I won't get a new job if I solve the code. There aren't any other jobs for women codebreakers. Solving the code is my job."

"But don't you want to get a headquarters job, like the Captain" Asha asked.

"No, I want to keep doing what I'm doing," replied Elizebeth. "I want to solve codes and make a difference in the world."

Elizebeth put the cardboard pieces back in the box. Next, she returned the box to the shelf. Then, she went back to the secret messages from the black leather case. She handed pages to Asha and Baz.

"So, what do codebreakers do during a war?" Asha asked.

Without taking her eyes off her paper, Elizebeth began to speak. "It is up to us—and our trainees—to stop things before they happen. We break down where things are, who is meeting, and where things are going. Then, we send that information to people who can stop bad things from happening."

Baz looked at the numbers on the paper. "How were these secret messages created?" he asked.

"Good question," said Elizebeth. "The secret

message creator uses a machine to type out the message. Then, the machine scrambles the message, turning the letters into numbers. On the receiving end, the person does the reverse to unscramble the message," she explained. She tapped her pencil on her secret message page. "The message creator and the message receiver have the same scramble/unscramble machine. We don't have their machine. So, we have to break the code by using our brains."

"Where do these secret messages come from?" Asha asked.

"The people who are on the other side of the war," replied Elizebeth. Asha looked at her paper, but her eyes jumped all over the page.

"To be a codebreaker, you must have patience and good concentration," said Elizebeth.

"It's like a game of chess," said Baz.

"Like any games, one must look for patterns," said Elizebeth.

Elizebeth moved her eyes back to her own page.

Asha and Baz settled into their work. Baz put all his focus on looking over his TOP SECRET ULTRA pages. Elizebeth sat across from him. She worked in silence. Using her pencil, she circled, underlined, and crossed out things. Her work was neat and logical.

Asha couldn't sit still. She looked up to spot birds chirping outside the window. She squirmed in her chair. She tapped her pencil on the desk.

"Having difficulty concentrating?" Elizebeth asked.

"I should get up," Asha suggested. "I work better if I can move around."

Baz nodded. He knew Asha had a hard time staying still.

"That's fine," said Elizebeth. "Codebreakers do more than examine secret messages." She once again rose to her feet and went over to the bookshelves. She dragged her finger across a row of books until she stopped at a great big book of maps. She brought it down and laid it on the other side of the desk.

"You might have a talent for research," she said to Asha. "Find me a map of the world."

Asha smiled, stood up, and started flipping through the pages of the book of maps. Elizebeth returned to her secret messages. She increased her speed in reading and writing. She was on to something.

It did not take long for Asha to find a map of the world.

"Here it is," Asha said, pointing to the map.

Nodding her head, Elizebeth said, "Good. Now locate Germany on the map for me."

"I can find Germany!" Baz broke in. He loved maps.

"I'm sure you can both find Germany," said Elizebeth.

"I got it, Baz," replied Asha. "I'm the researcher. You're the pattern finder."

Elizebeth tapped her pencil on her papers. "These messages were being sent to Germany," she said.

CHAPTER 5

SPIES

"**W**hy would spies be working for Germany?" asked Baz looking at the map.

"I know," Asha volunteered. "These spies are on the German side of the war." She straightened her back, knowing her answer was correct.

Baz smiled at his friend. He was proud she knew the answer. Elizebeth pointed to the map. "Now look for England. And then, the United States of America." Asha bent down and looked at the map again.

"I found England," Asha said as she pointed.

"And here's the United States," said Baz pointing to another place on the map.

"United States to England is a very important supply route," said Elizebeth. "Supply ships sail from the USA and travel across the Atlantic Ocean to England. Those supplies are then sent to people all over Europe."

"What kind of supplies are on the ships?" asked Asha.

"Medicine, clothing, food, blankets, extra help. All sorts of things," said Elizebeth.

Baz traced his finger from the United States across the ocean to England.

At that moment, Baz realized something. "The supply ships! What if the secret messages have something to do with the ships and the supply route?" he asked.

"A part of codebreaking is brainstorming," said Elizebeth. "Keep thinking. Why would the spies take interest in our supply ships and shipping routes?"

Asha's eyes widened. "The spies could track the supply ships. Then, they can send messages to tell their friends the locations," she said.

"If they know where the supply ships are, then they can sink them. That way, the supplies never reach England," said Elizebeth. "What happens if the other countries don't get medicine, clothes, food, or extra help?"

Baz put his hand up like he was in class. "Yes, Baz," said Elizebeth.

"The people in the other countries would get sick, freeze, starve, and wouldn't have any help," he replied.

Asha, Baz, and Elizebeth all went silent. They realized this was a very serious situation.

Elizebeth looked down at her pile of secret messages. "This is all part of breaking codes. Finding out who is sending messages. Figuring out who is receiving messages. Guessing what those messages might be about." She picked up her pencil once again and started making notes on the page.

At that moment, the front door opened. Elizebeth felt alarmed.

"William, is that you?" she asked. She covered her hands over the papers on her desk.

"Yes, dear," replied William. Elizebeth relaxed.

Asha and Baz looked down the hallway from the office.

William wore a dark suit and had a striped tie. "I spilled coffee on my shirt. I have to change," he said.

"OK," said Elizebeth. "I have some new codebreaker trainees here."

"Hello, new trainees. I'm William Friedman," William called out down the hallway. "Hello," Asha and Baz replied.

William went upstairs to change his shirt.

"Will he come help us?" Asha asked.

"No, William knows my projects are *Top Secret Ultra*. He won't come in the office while I'm working," replied Elizebeth.

Elizebeth, Asha, and Baz returned to their work.

"Excuse me," Baz spoke up. "You said you thought you were close to figuring out the code. What makes you think that?" In that moment, his love of puzzles was stronger than his nervousness.

"I'm seeing a pattern in the numbers," said Elizebeth. "The numbers look like a code I've encountered before."

"What was the key for that code?" asked Baz.

"Numbers replaced letters of the alphabet," said Elizebeth. "It was a reverse alphabet. There are 26 letters in the alphabet. Correct?" she asked.

"Correct," Asha and Baz replied.

"The other secret messages I solved used a backwards alphabet order. 26 = A. 25 = B. 24 = C," she explained.

"These secret messages are all numbers too," Baz pointed out. "What if they are using the backwards alphabet code with these messages? Let's test it out on a few lines of code."

"That's an idea. Good work," said Elizebeth. "Let's try using a backwards alphabet key." She used her pencil to switch a line of code from numbers to letters.

S	A	R	G	O
8	26	9	20	12

CHAPTER 6

SARGO

"**H**ow did you do that?" asked Asha.

"Using the backwards alphabet key," said Elizebeth.

Asha didn't understand. Baz scrunched up his face as he thought.

"A is the first letter of the alphabet," said Baz.

"With a backwards alphabet code, Z is the first letter in the alphabet," said Elizebeth.

"Could you write it down?" asked Asha.

Elizebeth took her pencil and wrote the letters of the alphabet.

ABCDEFGHIJKLMNOPQRSTUVWXYZ

"This is the alphabet, correct?" Elizebeth asked Asha and Baz.

"Correct," they replied.

"Then, if we reverse the order of the letters, the alphabet will be backwards," said Elizebeth. She wrote the alphabet backwards.

ZYXWVUTSRQPONMLKJIHGFEDCBA

"Backwards, Z is the first letter of the alphabet," said Elizebeth. "Z = 1, Y = 2, X = 3, and so on."

"Can I?" Baz asked Elizebeth, reaching for her pencil.

Baz wrote the numbers 1 to 26 under Elizebeth's backwards alphabet. The letters and numbers looked like this:

Z	Y	X	W	V	U	T	S	R	Q	P	O	N
1	2	3	4	5	6	7	8	9	10	11	12	13

M	L	K	J	I	H	G	F	E	D	C	B	A
14	15	16	17	18	19	20	21	22	23	24	25	26

Asha looked for the letter S on the backwards alphabet. According to the backwards alphabet key, S = 8. She looked at all the numbers on the secret message again. She pointed to every number and its matching letter in the backwards alphabet.

8 26 9 20 12 = S A R G O

"It spells SARGO!" said Asha. "SARGO doesn't make any sense. We must have the wrong key." She shook her head.

"Now we need to connect it to the five Ws," said Elizebeth.

"What are the five Ws?" Asha asked.

"The five questions for problem solving," explained Elizebeth. "Who, what, when, where, and why."

Asha and Baz leaned in.

"We can ask ourselves," explained Elizebeth. "Who is Sargo? What is Sargo? When is Sargo? Where is Sargo? Why is Sargo?"

"And if we figure out if Sargo is a who, what, when, or why, we will know if Sargo is a person, place, or thing," said Baz. "We solve the problem."

"Let's go through all the messages and underline each time we see the numbers 8, 26, 9, 20, 12," Elizebeth proposed. "That way, we will see how often we find Sargo."

"That is a pattern," said Baz. "Numbers repeating is a pattern."

"Yes, it is," said Elizebeth.

Asha split the pages of secret messages. Elizebeth and Baz each took a small pile of papers. With pencils in their hands, they scanned the typewritten numbers for 8, 26, 9, 20, 12.

The warm afternoon sun shone through the window beside Elizebeth's desk.

"Got one," said Baz. He underlined the numbers.

"Me too," said Elizebeth. They each handed their underlined pages to Asha. She put them in a pile on the desk.

Elizebeth and Baz continued underlining numbers on pages.

"I'm seeing a pattern," Elizebeth finally said, looking up from her pile of secret messages.

"What is it?" asked Asha.

"It's always on the last line," said Baz.

He pointed to the bottom of his paper. "The last line of every message is 8, 26, 9, 20, 12."

Asha flipped through the pile of papers. She confirmed the last line on every page had an underline from either Elizebeth or Baz.

"It's another step in breaking the code," Baz clapped.

Elizebeth smiled at her codebreaking trainees.

"So, we know those numbers equal Sargo. And Sargo is a word that appears on the last line of every secret message," said Baz.

"Let's do the five Ws," Asha suggested. "Sargo is on the last line of every page. Is Sargo a who, what, where, when, or why?"

Baz tapped his finger on his chin as he thought.

"It's not a where or when because that doesn't make sense to be on the last line of every message," he decided. "Imagine ending every secret message with *kitchen* or *4 p.m.*"

"What if Sargo were a what?" Asha wondered out loud. "Would you finish every message with a what? Like *box* or *cup*."

"No," said Baz.

"Think about when you write a letter to

someone. What do you write as the last line?" Elizebeth asked Asha and Baz.

Asha needed to pretend to write a letter. She took an invisible pencil in her hand and wrote on an imaginary paper in the air. Baz looked on with interest. Asha was always so creative. She finished the letter and let her invisible pencil disappear into the air.

"My name," she declared. "The last line of a letter always finishes with my name. *From, Asha* or *Love, Asha.*" Her face beamed with pride.

"That means," Baz said looking down at the messages, "Sargo can be a who." He looked up at Elizebeth for approval. She smiled and nodded her head.

"You are right. Sargo is a who. The code name of a spy," she said.

Asha and Baz gasped in shock. They had uncovered the code name of a spy sending secret messages during World War II.

"How do you know Sargo is a spy?" asked Asha.

At that moment, they heard steps on the stairs.

"Dear, I left my watch in your office last night," William called out from the hallway.

He did not walk into the office. He stayed in the hallway. He put his hand in front of his eyes. Elizebeth looked around the room for the watch. Baz noticed it on top of the fireplace. "There it is," Baz pointed.

Elizebeth picked up the watch. She walked to the hallway and handed it to William. Her husband kept his hand over his eyes.

"Thank you, dear, I'll see you tonight," he said. He kissed her cheek. Then, he turned and walked out the front door.

"Have a nice day," Elizebeth said to her husband. She closed the door behind him.

"Is your husband shy like me?" asked Baz when she returned to the office.

"William is not shy," explained Elizebeth. "He covers his eyes so he doesn't see my secret work."

Elizebeth bent to get the black leather case under her desk. She took out a brown notebook. She flipped through the pages.

"How do you know Sargo is a spy?" Asha asked again.

"When I decode a message with a spy name, I put it on a list," said Elizebeth.

She flipped to the last page and showed the codebreaker trainees a list of names.

Carré
Jordan
Kopkow
Kowalewski
Lella
Rader
Sargo
Tingling
Witherington

Asha pointed to Sargo. "It really is a name," she said. "It looks like we have cracked the code!"

Elizebeth nodded and smiled.

Baz pointed at the secret messages and jumped up and down. "Oh my gosh! The secret message key really is a backwards alphabet!" he said.

Asha and Baz gave each other a high five.

"You did it, Elizebeth!" they cheered.

"*We* did it," Elizebeth replied.

"We have done some good work, codebreaker

trainees," said Elizebeth. "What do we know so far?"

"The spies are using a backwards alphabet key," said Asha.

"Spies are working for the the bad guys," said Baz.

"And we guess spies are watching the shipping routes," added Asha.

"This is good," Elizebeth nodded.

"We know there's a spy with the code name Sargo," said Asha.

"What's the next step?" Baz asked, leaning on the desk. He felt the hairs on his arms stand up.

Elizebeth got up and walked over to the fireplace. She placed her hands on her hips. For a moment, she paused to think.

"See," Asha whispered to Baz. "I'm not the only one who has to change positions to think better."

Asha and Baz moved away from the desk to the center of the room. After a while, Elizebeth began to speak.

"We broke the code," she said. Asha started pacing to help focus her brain.

"The key is a backwards alphabet. And we have 28 pages of secret messages," she said after counting the number of papers. "That means we have 28 secret messages to unlock," she began. "Asha, take a piece of paper and copy the code again. That way Baz and I will each have a code key. Then, we will go through each secret message and decode them one by one."

Baz hurried to his seat and began looking at the papers. Asha picked up the yellow notepad and started writing the key.

"We have 28 messages to break as soon as possible," Elizebeth said, tapping on her pile of pages.

CHAPTER 7

28 MESSAGES

"The spies have made a big mistake using the same secret code for their messages," Elizebeth said.

"How is it a mistake?" Baz asked.

"They should change the code every day so it's harder to break," she explained. "A way to break codes is to find mistakes."

"Their mistake is our opportunity," said Asha.

At that moment, there was a loud knock at the door. Asha and Baz sat on the desk to hide the secret messages. Elizebeth nodded. She put her finger up to her lips. "Shhh," she said.

She walked down the hallway and opened the door.

The man in the Navy uniform was back. He looked even angrier than before.

"You again, Captain," she said.

"Any updates?" he asked. He tapped his foot.

"Nothing I'm ready to share yet," said Elizebeth.

"I need—" he yelled and then stopped himself. He fixed his tie and lowered his voice. He looked side to side to be sure no one was listening. "I mean, *we* need, that code broken immediately, Mrs. Friedman," he growled.

Baz listened and felt terrible. This is why he didn't like speaking up. If you said the wrong thing, people would get mad.

"Codebreaking takes patience," said Elizebeth.

The Captain's face went purple with anger. "I don't think you understand how important this is to my career!" he barked.

"Yelling at me doesn't help break the code," replied Elizebeth. "And breathing down my neck won't get the problem solved any faster."

"I will fire you," warned the Captain.

"You can't fire me. Only an Admiral can fire me. And you are not an Admiral," said Elizebeth. The Captain looked crushed. "Now excuse me, but I have work to do." She nodded her head, then closed the door.

"Back to work," she called out as she walked down the hallway.

"Why didn't you tell him we had broken Sargo?" Asha asked.

"I didn't tell him about Sargo because it's not enough yet," said Elizebeth. She looked Asha and Baz in the eyes. "Also, he's a bully." She winked at the codebreaker trainees.

Baz liked her courage. Elizebeth had stood up to her bully.

They settled into their chairs. They replaced the numbers with letters. One by one. Soon, the letters formed words. The words formed sentences. Then, the sentences made entire secret messages.

Elizebeth and Baz sat like statues working on their secret messages. Asha jiggled her legs. Elizebeth and Baz looked at Asha.

"Sorry, I can't help it," said Asha.

"She's a mover." Baz smiled, trying to make Asha feel more comfortable.

Elizebeth nodded her head. She understood. "Asha, there is more research to do, if you like," Elizebeth offered.

"Yes, please," said Asha.

Elizebeth pointed to the shelves behind her. "Look for a book about ships. When you find it, search for a ship called the *Queen Mary*."

"OK," agreed Asha.

She walked over to the white, wooden bookshelves and skimmed the book titles. There were thin books on plays. There were thick books on someone named William Shakespeare. There were new books on wheat, old books on the moon, and much more.

Finally, Asha found a big, blue book on ships. It took both her hands to lift it off the bookshelf and carry it to the desk.

She opened the cover. The pages smelled like the sea. She flipped the pages to the table of contents. It was in alphabetical order. She dragged her finger down the page until she read the words: the *Queen Mary*.

"Found it," Asha said to Elizebeth and Baz.

"Well done," said Elizebeth, looking up from her page. "My secret messages keep referring to a ship named the *Queen Mary*. Do yours?" Elizebeth asked Baz.

"Yes," he replied with a serious face.

"Why do you think the *Queen Mary* is a ship.

The messages could be about *Queen Mary* the person," said Baz.

"There was a Queen Mary. In fact, there were two Queens of England named Mary," said Elizebeth. "But they both lived a long, long time ago. There is no reason for them to be in a secret message today."

Asha flipped to the page about the ship named the *Queen Mary*. She read aloud, "Ship builders began construction on the *Queen Mary* in the 1930s in Scotland. The book says it's the greatest ship that ever sailed. At the beginning, it carried rich and famous people on vacations."

Asha looked at the picture of the *Queen Mary*.

"It's a big, steel ship with many windows. There are three round smokestacks and four big propellers," she read.

Baz leaned in to listen to Asha.

"The ship's nickname is 'the Gray Ghost,'" said Asha. "It's painted gray in the picture."

Baz and Elizebeth stopped what they were doing and joined Asha looking at the ship's picture.

"I bet a gray ship like that would be hard to see in the fog or at night," suggested Baz. Asha nodded her head.

"I've read about this ship," Elizebeth realized. "It's very fast."

"It's a supply ship for the war," Asha read.

Baz started biting his lip.

"What's wrong, Baz?" Asha asked. "He always bites his lip when he's worried," she explained to Elizebeth.

Baz looked down at the picture of the ship. And then looked up to face Elizebeth and Asha.

"We know these secret messages are from a spy named Sargo," he began. "Sargo is writing about the *Queen Mary*. And the *Queen Mary* is a supply ship for the war."

He looked at Elizebeth.

She nodded her head. "Keep going," she encouraged.

"Why is Sargo interested in the *Queen Mary*?" he asked.

Asha's body went stiff and her face turned white. "It's a supply ship," she whispered.

Asha pulled out the map they had been looking at before. She pointed to the Atlantic Ocean.

"The *Queen Mary* is a supply ship traveling from the United States to England," Asha said. "What...what happens if the ship doesn't make it to England?" she asked.

Elizebeth's face turned white as well. "England needs the supplies aboard that ship. If something were to happen to the *Queen Mary*, well, England would..." Elizebeth paused to take a breath. "England would be out of the war."

"I saw something..." said Elizebeth. She rushed back to her desk and sorted through the piles of secret messages. She was looking for something. One secret message deep in the papers.

She took hold of her pencil and began switching the numbers to letters on that page.

"What's she doing?" Baz asked Asha.

"She's decoding another secret message," said Asha.

They moved closer to Elizebeth.

Finally, Elizebeth put down her pencil. She took a deep breath. Elizebeth looked worried.

"What does that secret message say?" asked Asha.

Elizebeth turned the page to Asha and Baz.

T H E R E   A R E   8 . 0 0 0
7 19 22 9 22   26 9 22   8 . 0 0 0

S O L D I E R S   S A I L I N G
8 12 15 23 18 22 9 8   8 26 18 15 18 13 20

O N   T H E   Q U E E N   M A R Y .
12 13   7 19 22   10 6 22 22 13   14 26 9 2 .

W E   O F F E R   A
4 22   12 21 21 22 9   26

$ 2 5 0 . 0 0 0	R E W A R D	T O
$ 2 5 0 . 0 0 0	9 22 4 26 9 23	7 12

A N Y	C A P T A I N	W H O
26 13 2	24 26 11 7 26 18 13	4 19 12

S I N K S	T H E	S H I P .
8 18 13 16 8	7 19 22	8 19 18 11 .

Asha and Baz froze.

"We have to save the *Queen Mary*," Baz whispered.

"Yes," agreed Asha, "but how?"

CHAPTER 8

THE QUEEN MARY

Elizebeth jumped to her feet. "I have to call the Captain," she said. She walked out of the room toward a phone in the front hall.

"The Captain of the *Queen Mary*?" Baz asked Asha.

"No, the Navy Captain who keeps coming to the door," said Asha. "She broke the code."

"What are we going to do?" Baz worried.

They heard Elizebeth dial the phone. "Hello, Captain," she began. Asha heard her say "*Queen Mary*" and "sink" and "$250,000 reward" and then, "goodbye."

Elizebeth walked down the hall. She stood in the doorway with her hands on her hips. She looked past Asha and Baz to the light coming in through the window. Baz tapped his fingers on his arm while he waited for Elizebeth to come up with a plan.

"I have told the Captain that the *Queen Mary* is in danger," said Elizebeth. "He wants more information and to be updated as soon as possible."

"What should we do now?" asked Asha.

"We have given the Captain very good information. It is a good start to saving the *Queen Mary*," said Elizebeth.

Elizebeth moved her eyes from the windows and set them on Asha. "The spies don't know we have discovered their error. They sent 28 messages using the same key. We have broken the secret code. We will use it to our advantage."

Elizebeth walked over to the pile of coded messages on the desk.

"Baz, I have a new job for you," said Elizebeth. "Go through these pages again. We know that 10, 6, 22, 22, 13 and 14, 26, 9, 2, stand for QUEEN MARY. Look for those numbers. We need to see if we can uncover any more information."

Baz and Elizebeth rushed back to the wooden desk. They focused their attention on the pages and got to work.

"What should I do?" Asha asked.

"We need you to organize the papers as we go through them," said Elizebeth. "Codebreakers must be very organized."

Baz found 10, 6, 22, 22, 13 and 14, 26, 9, 2 on several pages. He underlined them and handed them to Asha. She handed them one by one to Elizebeth. Then, Elizebeth went through each line of numbers and letters.

One message caught Elizebeth's attention. She replaced every number with a letter from the backwards alphabet. Then, she drew a star in the top right corner of the paper.

"This secret message is important," she said. "The *Queen Mary* left the United States on March 8th at 6 p.m.," said Elizebeth. Asha handed another of Baz's papers to Elizebeth.

Elizebeth worked without a word. Baz stopped what he was doing and watched her. Again, Elizebeth drew a star in the corner of the page.

"The spies are tracking the ship. This message reports the *Queen Mary* was off the coast of

South America. On March 12th at 3 p.m.," said Elizebeth. She held out her hand to Asha to get another paper. "Keep this one safe," she said to Asha. Asha put the latest message with the star on the corner of the desk.

"The messages give the date and time?" asked Asha.

"Oh yes," said Elizebeth. "Remember: who, what, when, where, and why."

"That's the last message," said Asha. She pointed down to an empty spot on the desk.

"What now?" Baz asked Elizebeth.

"We update the Captain," Elizebeth said. "We have the who, what, when, where, and why. The bad guys have offered a $250,000 reward to sink the Queen Mary. On March 12th at 3 p.m., the Queen Mary was off the coast of South America. The spies are tracking its route. The Captain needs to let the ship know they are in danger."

Baz and Asha nodded at the information. "OK," they said at the same time.

Elizebeth turned and walked back to the phone in the front hall.

Baz started pacing back and forth in the room. He walked from the window to the doorway and back again. After a while, it started to get on his best friend's nerves.

"Can you stop?" Asha asked.

"I can't help it. I'm nervous," he replied. "What if they sink the *Queen Mary*?"

Asha put her hands on his shoulders. "Breathe," she suggested. "You are getting stressed out. Breathe."

He took a long, deep breath. It felt good to have the pressure of her hands push on his shoulders. "It will be fine. It will be fine," Baz repeated to himself.

After a while, Elizebeth walked back down the hallway and into the office.

"Well?" asked Baz.

"We did a good job," she smiled. "The Captain is sending a radio signal to the ship right now. He says the *Queen Mary* has enough time to change its sailing route and get to safety. We have saved the *Queen Mary*."

Elizebeth patted Asha and Baz on their shoulders.

"He also thinks he'll get his promotion now," she moaned. Then, she smiled at Asha and Baz.

"You are good codebreakers. Thank you for your help," she said.

Asha and Baz jumped for joy!

This gave Asha an idea. "Elizebeth," she began, "Baz and I have a secret message we have to break for school. Um, I mean another project," she winked at Baz. "Do you think you could help us solve the code?'

"I don't see why not," Elizebeth replied. "But let's get some fresh air. We will work on your secret message outside."

CHAPTER 9

FINDING THE KEY

Elizebeth cleaned up her desk and put all her papers away in the black leather cases. She locked them and hid them under her desk.

"Don't you get tired of hiding your work?" asked Asha.

"I am used to it," Elizebeth explained.

She walked them out of the office. Through the kitchen. Then, out to the back garden.

Four great big leafy trees stood at the bottom of the yard. A cloth hammock hung between two of the trees.

At the other end of the yard stood the house.

It had a wooden porch and a screened-in room at the back. Green ivy grew up the sides of the two-story home. The wooden frames of the square windows were white like the front door.

Elizebeth led them to the hammock and two chairs.

"Sit," she invited them.

Both Asha and Baz stepped forward to sit on the hammock. "You first," Baz offered. "We can share," Asha replied with a smile.

The two friends held on to the hammock and sat down. Their legs dangled above the ground.

"Ouch, wait a minute," Asha said. The magic stick was in her pocket and it poked her leg. She took the magic stick out and placed it on her lap for safekeeping.

"That's an unusual stick," noticed Elizebeth as she sat in a chair.

"It's pretty magical," said Baz. Asha laughed.

"So, tell me about your secret message," invited Elizebeth.

Baz reached into his pocket and pulled out the worksheet. He made the hammock swing.

"Careful," warned Asha, grabbing the hammock to steady it.

He held out the worksheet Ms. Wilson had given to them in class.

Elizebeth took the paper from Baz and read it over. She read the instructions aloud. "Solve the letter/number key below to decode the secret message."

"So, what have you learned today about breaking secret messages?" she asked.

Asha raised her hand like she was in class. "No need to raise your hand," Elizebeth said, sitting back in her chair.

"Secret messages can be numbers. Numbers can replace letters of the alphabet," said Asha.

"And there's a key to the code," added Baz. "If you find the key, you can unlock the code."

"We used the backwards alphabet key to decode the secret messages," Asha said.

"Maybe we can use a backwards alphabet key for our secret code too," said Baz.

Asha looked at the key Ms. Wilson had provided. "Hey, wait a minute," Asha said looking down at the key. "There are already some numbers here." She pointed down at the paper to show Baz and Elizebeth.

"I saw that," said Elizebeth. "There is a pattern there."

Baz looked down at the worksheet. "There is a pattern of 5, 10, 15, 20, and 25 in the key. Does that still work with the backwards alphabet?"

Asha counted the alphabet on her fingers. "V is the fifth letter of the backwards alphabet," she exclaimed. Then, she continued counting. "Q is the tenth letter of the backwards alphabet!"

"That's it," said Baz sitting up straighter. "Each number equals the letter placement in the alphabet. It works! We discovered the key!"

"That must be it!" Asha cheered.

"Slow down," said Elizebeth. "You haven't

tested the key on the message yet! The alphabet can be forward or backwards in secret messages."

Asha moved too fast. The hammock began to swing, and they both fell off.

"Goodness, are you all right?" asked Elizebeth.

Asha and Baz broke into laughter.

"We're fine," said Asha.

She got to her knees and then stood up. She held her hand out to Baz and helped him to his feet.

"Thank you for your help, Elizebeth," said Asha.

"No, thank you," replied Elizebeth. "You were very helpful in solving the 28 secret messages."

"We have to get back," exclaimed Baz. He grabbed Asha's hand and began pulling her.

"Good luck with your work," Asha called out as they ran along the grass to the small patch of sand.

"Goodbye," Elizebeth called out behind them.

"What if she sees us time travel?" Asha asked Baz. They looked back to Elizebeth. But she wasn't in the chair anymore. She had walked up the other side of the grass along the path toward the front of the house. Seconds later she was out of sight.

"We have to get back to school," said Asha.

Baz folded up the worksheet and put it in his pocket.

"Do you want to draw our school in the sand?" asked Asha, holding out the magic stick to Baz. "No, thank you," Baz declined, holding up his hands.

Asha bent down and drew a picture of their school.

"Get in," she said to Baz. He bit his lip. He still felt a little nervous using the magic stick. He stepped inside the drawing.

Winds from the south turned the sand into a gentle tornado. Asha and Baz traveled through space and time.

Then, the mini tornado blew away. Asha and Baz looked around. The house and trees were gone. Instead, they were standing in the schoolyard.

The school bell rang. The other kids rushed to the back door of the school. Asha and Baz raced. They filed through the door, walked down the hall, straight to their classroom. Asha put the magic stick in her backpack for safekeeping.

She met Baz at their desks.

"Ready to solve a secret message and win a reward?" Baz asked as he winked.

"You know I am!" said Asha.

"Let's break this code," said Baz. He took the worksheet out of his pocket and put it on his desk. He and Asha sat in their chairs. The two friends worked together filling in the blanks of the secret message key.

CHAPTER 10

BREAKING THE CODE

"**Z** = 1, Y = 2, X = 3, that's the backwards alphabet code," Baz whispered as he read over the Codebreaker Challenge. Asha looked around to ensure no one was listening in. They were safe. The other teams were deep in thought working on their worksheets.

Ms. Wilson sat at her desk grading tests.

"We have the key to break the code," said Asha. "So, we need to write the letters above the numbers in the secret message."

"The letters will create words. And the words will make a sentence," said Baz. It was like decoding the secret message with Elizebeth Friedman.

The Codebreaker Challenge

Instructions: Solve the letter/number key below to decode the secret message.

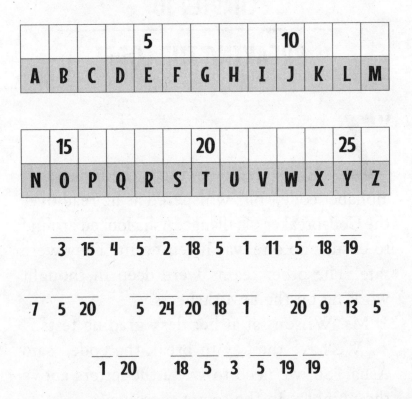

			5						10			
A	B	C	D	E	F	G	H	I	J	K	L	M

	15				20				25			
N	O	P	Q	R	S	T	U	V	W	X	Y	Z

3 15 4 5 2 18 5 1 11 5 18 19

7 5 20   5 24 20 18 1   20 9 13 5

1 20   18 5 3 5 19 19

"The first letters," Asha said pointing to the numbers in the first line.

3 15 4 5

"That spells..." Baz said, writing the backwards alphabet.

XLWV

"That makes no sense," he said.

"But that's the key to the secret message," said Asha. "What are we missing?"

Baz looked at the challenge.

"In the instructions Ms. Wilson has written 5 = E," said Baz. "We must have the key wrong."

They both thought for a moment.

"Elizebeth said the alphabet can be forward or backwards in secret messages," Baz said.

Asha counted the backwards alphabet on her fingers.

$$Z = 1$$
$$Y = 2$$
$$X = 3$$
$$W = 4$$
$$V = 5$$

"In the backwards alphabet, V = 5," said Asha. "So, it can't be a backwards alphabet because according to the paper Ms. Wilson gave us, 5 = E."

Asha counted again.

A = 1
B = 2
C = 3
D = 4
E = 5

"In the alphabet where the letters go forward, E = 5," she said.

"That's it," said Baz. "The secret message key is the regular alphabet."

He filled out the key.

1	2	3	4	5	6	7	8	9	10	11	12	13
A	B	C	D	E	F	G	H	I	J	K	L	M

14	15	16	17	18	19	20	21	22	23	24	25	26
N	O	P	Q	R	S	T	U	V	W	X	Y	Z

Then, he focused on the secret message numbers.

$$\overline{3}\ \overline{15}\ \overline{4}\ \overline{5}\ \overline{2}\ \overline{18}\ \overline{5}\ \overline{1}\ \overline{11}\ \overline{5}\ \overline{18}\ \overline{19}$$

$$\overline{7}\ \overline{5}\ \overline{20}\quad \overline{5}\ \overline{24}\ \overline{20}\ \overline{18}\ \overline{1}\quad \overline{20}\ \overline{9}\ \overline{13}\ \overline{5}$$

$$\overline{1}\ \overline{20}\quad \overline{18}\ \overline{5}\ \overline{3}\ \overline{5}\ \overline{19}\ \overline{19}$$

3 15 4 5 = CODE

"That's a word," said Asha. She felt excited. "The first part of the first word is CODE!"

"Shhh!" said Baz, looking around the class. "Don't let them know we know."

Baz tapped his finger on the second set of numbers. "You try now," he encouraged Asha.

2 18 5 1 11 5 18 19

Asha broke the code.

BREAKERS

"We are doing it," said Asha with pride.

Asha and Baz worked one row at a time until they had solved the secret message.

When they finished, they gave each other a high five.

The clap of hands made everyone look up. Including Ms. Wilson.

"Do you have something to show me?" she asked.

Asha and Baz felt excited. Ms. Wilson motioned for them to come to the front of the class.

Asha stood up. Baz sunk down in his seat. "Asha, you can present for your team," said Ms. Wilson smiling at shy Baz. He flushed red and mouthed "thank you" to his teacher.

Asha picked up the worksheet and walked to the front of the class.

First, she showed the paper to Ms. Wilson. Their teacher looked over their work.

"Congratulations, team Asha and Baz. You have solved the Codebreaker Challenge!"

There were cheers of applause, but also a few boos of jealousy.

"Cheers only, thank you," Ms. Wilson said as she frowned. She turned her attention to Asha.

"Could you please explain how you solved the secret message," said Ms. Wilson.

Asha took a deep breath and stood a little taller. She loved being the center of attention. She spoke so that everyone could hear. She moved her head around and looked everyone in the eye as she spoke.

Asha explained how they had to look for patterns within the letter/number key. She described how they had to be patient. She explained looking for who, what, where, when, and why.

"So, what is the secret message?" asked a student. The class was on the edge of their seats.

"No, I want to know what the reward is," a boy yelled from the back.

"The secret message reveals the reward," said Ms. Wilson.

"Baz, would you be comfortable writing out the decoded message on the board?" asked Ms. Wilson. "You don't have to say a word."

The whole class looked at Baz. He blushed deep red. Asha ran over to him. "Remember, Elizebeth found the courage to stand up to the Captain. You can find the courage to stand in front of the class."

"I can't do it," said Baz.

"Yes, you can," encouraged Asha.

He looked around the room. Asha held out her hand. He took it.

"I'm right here with you," said Asha.

He found the courage to walk to the front of the class.

Ms. Wilson nodded and smiled in support. The kids didn't make fun of him. They clapped in support.

His hand shook as he wrote the numbers on the board. Above the numbers he wrote the letters. It wasn't his best writing because he was so nervous, but he did it.

"Good job," said Ms. Wilson. Baz bolted back to his seat.

C	O	D	E	B	R	E	A	K	E	R	S
3	15	4	5	2	18	5	1	11	5	18	19

G	E	T		E	X	T	R	A		T	I	M	E
7	5	20		5	24	20	18	1		20	9	13	5

A	T		R	E	C	E	S	S
1	20		18	5	3	5	19	19

"CODEBREAKERS GET EXTRA TIME AT RECESS," read Ms. Wilson.

"No fair," groaned a boy.

"Asha and Baz win the challenge," said Ms. Wilson. "They have extra time at the next recess."

Asha skipped back to her chair beside Baz.

"What was your greatest help in cracking the code?" asked Ms. Wilson.

"Elizebeth Friedman," replied Asha.

"The famous American codebreaker?" said Ms. Wilson, impressed to hear the name.

"Who's that?" asked a girl.

"Is she a supply teacher?" asked another student.

"Elizebeth Friedman taught herself how to break secret messages. And then she trained others how to do it. Let's see if we can find her," Ms. Wilson said as she took out her laptop and searched for Elizebeth Friedman.

"She worked for a lot of government departments. The U.S. Coast Guard, the Navy, and the FBI," Ms. Wilson read. "She broke up crime rings and helped to capture spies."

"That's Elizebeth," Baz whispered to Asha.

"Back to our codebreaking challenge." Ms. Wilson redirected the class. "What skills do you need to break secret messages?"

Hands shot up all around the class.

"Reading and writing," said a girl.

"Problem solving," volunteered a boy.

"Organization," said a student.

"Well done," smiled Ms. Wilson. "Should we do another challenge next week?" she asked.

"Yes," cheered the class.

Ms. Wilson always created the best class challenges.

APPENDIX

Are secret codes real?

Yes, secret codes are real. People, businesses, and countries put codes on their secret information to protect it.

Here are some examples of secret codes:
- bank card numbers
- credit card numbers
- computer passwords
- email passwords

Was Elizebeth Friedman a real person?

Yes, Elizebeth Friedman was a real person. Her story with Asha and Baz is fiction. Here are some facts about her life:
- Born Elizebeth Smith in 1892, she was the youngest of nine children.
- Elizebeth's mother didn't want anyone to call her daughter "Eliza" as a nickname. So, she spelled her daughter's name "Elizebeth" instead of "Elizabeth."
- Elizebeth graduated from Hillsdale College.

- She worked as a high school principal for a year.
- She married her husband, William, in May 1917.
- The Friedmans had two children: a son and a daughter.
- In 1921, the Friedmans went to work for the War Department in Washington, D.C.
- Elizebeth used her skills to break secret codes to catch gangsters and spies.
- She cracked the code to save the *Queen Mary* during World War II.
- Elizebeth Friedman worked for the U.S. Navy and other government departments.
- Elizebeth Smith Friedman died on October 31, 1980, in Plainfield, New Jersey. She was 88 years old.
- Elizebeth Friedman was a pioneer in codebreaking.
- Elizebeth's projects were TOP SECRET ULTRA.
- She never shared any of the secrets of her projects, even when others took credit for her work.

Was Sargo a real person?

Yes, Sargo was a real person. He was a spy. Here are a few facts about his life:

- His name was Johannes Siegfried Becker.
- Sargo was his code name.
- He was one of the head spies in South America during World War II.

Was the *Queen Mary* a real ship?

Yes, the *Queen Mary* was a real ship. Here are some facts about the ship:

- In 1930, construction on the *Queen Mary* began in Scotland.
- The first voyage of the *Queen Mary* was on May 27, 1936.
- The ship had five dining areas, two bars, two swimming pools, one ballroom, and one squash court.
- The *Queen Mary* was a very fast ship.
- During World War II, the *Queen Mary* sailed as a supply ship. It carried over 810,000 military personnel back and forth across the Atlantic Ocean.
- The German side of the war offered a $250,000 reward to any Captain who could destroy the *Queen Mary*.

- In 1947, after the war, the *Queen Mary* returned to being a cruise ship.
- It retired from sea voyage in 1967.
- The *Queen Mary* is now a tourist attraction. It is in Southern California.

TYPES OF SECRET CODES AND CIPHERS

- Morse code (spaced dots and dashes replace letters of the alphabet):

.... / .. ... / .- / -- --- -. ... . /
-. --- -.. . / . .-.. . -- -- -. ... .

(This is a Morse code example.)

- Caesar code (a letter of the alphabet shifted down in placement replaces a letter):

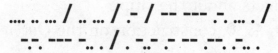

(This is a Caesar code example.)

- Pigpen cipher (a symbol replaces a letter of the alphabet):

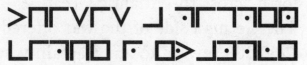

(This is a Pigpen cipher example.)

Acknowledgment

With thanks to Kirsten Marion, Dharmali Patel, Emily Stewart, Debbie Greenberg, and David Moratto for their talented contributions to the Asha and Baz Series.

Coming Next!

ASHA and BAZ
Meet Katia Krafft

(Book 4)
By
Caroline Fernandez

*Asha and Baz must create an eruption
for the Great Volcano Challenge!*

CHAPTER 1

THE GREAT VOLCANO CHALLENGE

Science class had been building up to the Great Volcano Challenge all week. Each team now had supplies to build their own volcano. "This might get messy," Ms. Wilson warned.

"Does everyone have a partner?" she asked. Ms. Wilson looked around the room. There was a range of reactions. Some kids responded with a "yes." Others gave a thumbs up. A few nodded.

Baz was one of the students who nodded. He was too shy to do anything bolder.

His best friend, Asha, was outgoing. She

gave all three reactions. "Yes," she yelled, then she motioned a thumbs-up, and finally she finished with a larger-than-life head nod.

"You don't have to do all that," whispered Baz to Asha. His cheeks blushed. He sank in his chair.

"It's fine," said Asha. She enjoyed getting attention.

"You know, I've lived through a volcano eruption," said Ms. Wilson. "In 2010, a volcano erupted in Iceland. It blew ash all over Europe. I got stuck in France because they closed all the airports."

The Great Volcano Challenge was a project and a competition. The teams had to build their own volcano using the supplies on their table. The team that had the best volcanic eruption would get a real-life lava rock.

Asha wanted the lava rock. It sat on Ms. Wilson's desk. It was a dull black color. It had a circle shape. It had tiny holes all over it, like a sponge. Asha wondered if it was as light as a sponge. Her fingers tingled to touch it.

"I want to win," Asha said to Baz.

"I'm not sure we can win this one," he said. "This looks like an impossible challenge."

He picked up the worksheet. Then, he read it to Asha.

The Great Volcano Challenge

Build a volcano. Then, create a volcanic eruption.
 Supplies:
- **White vinegar**
- **Baking soda**
- **Dish soap**
- **Empty plastic water bottle**
- **Small funnel**
- **Tablespoon**
- **Measuring cup**
- **Pie plate**
- **Clean cloth**

"There aren't any measurements," said Baz. He felt panic in his tummy.

"How do we build a volcano out of all this?" asked a student.

"Think about it," said Ms. Wilson. "What is the shape of a volcano? What is inside a volcano? What happens when a volcano erupts?"

The class broke out into discussions and brainstorming.

One team tried stacking the supplies to build a volcano.

"That looks like a tower, not a volcano," whispered Baz to Asha.

"Is this it?" asked a student on that team.

"Keep trying," said Ms. Wilson.

Another team combined all the vinegar and baking soda. It made a huge mess of fizz and bubbles on their table.

"That's an eruption, but not a volcano," whispered Asha to Baz.

"Keep trying," said Ms. Wilson. "And clean up, please."

The room smelled like vinegar.

Baz inspected each volcano supply on their table. "This doesn't make any sense," he said.

He leaned in to speak to Asha so the other teams wouldn't hear.

"These supplies don't have anything to do with volcanoes," said Baz.

Asha pointed to the plastic water bottle. "This one might," she said.

"What do you mean?" asked Baz.

"Ms. Wilson gave us a clue. What is the shape of a volcano?"

"I don't understand," said Baz.

"Use your imagination," said Asha. "Volcanoes have the shape of mountains. Water bottles have a mountain shape."

Baz and Asha studied the water bottle.

"You're right!" Baz replied. "The water bottle is a volcano shape."

"Now what?" asked Asha.

Then, the recess bell rang out. "Leave everything where it is," Ms. Wilson said in a loud voice. "We are going to continue the Great Volcano Challenge after recess."

"We need the stick," Baz whispered to Asha.

The students left their volcano supplies. They walked to their backpacks to get their snacks and outside toys. But not Asha and Baz. They walked over to Asha's backpack and dug out the special stick. They smiled at each other, knowing that an adventure was coming.

They had found it in the schoolyard. Whenever they used this stick, they went back in time. The stick was as long as the area between Asha's wrist and elbow. It was a dark chocolate-brown color at one end. At the other end, it was a warm honey-yellow color. This was no ordinary wooden stick.

So far, it had taken them to see a rocket

scientist, an inventor, and a codebreaker. All from different times and places.

"Do you think the stick knows anything about volcanoes?" Asha asked Baz as they walked out of the school building. "I bet it does," Baz said, biting his bottom lip. He always bit his lip when he was nervous.

The kids broke into a run. They headed for the edge of the playground where the grass met the sand.

"You do it this time," Asha said, holding out the stick to Baz. He took two steps back and held out his hands in protest. "Hard no. Nope," he replied.

"You don't need to be afraid of it," said Asha.

Baz held his hands up and said, "I'm not afraid of it. I don't trust it." They both broke into fits of laughter.

"Fine," said Asha.

She sat on the sand. She used the magic stick to draw a volcano.

"Wait for me," said Baz and he jumped onto the volcano with Asha. She touched the stick to the sand and yelled, "Erupt!"

In that exact moment, the south wind blew

a mini tornado around them. Asha and Baz traveled through space and time.

"Are we there yet?" Baz yelled with his hands up over his eyes. "We are somewhere," said Asha.

They looked down at the ground. The volcano drawing was gone. Written in its place was a name and a year:

KATIA KRAFFT. 1973.